ULTIMATE

TESLA MODEL S

By Amy C. Rea

Kaleidoscope
Minneapolis, MN

BIGFOOT BOOKS

The Quest for Discovery Never Ends

This edition is co-published by agreement between Kaleidoscope and World Book, Inc.

Kaleidoscope Publishing, Inc.
6012 Blue Circle Drive
Minnetonka, MN 55343 U.S.A.

World Book, Inc.
180 North LaSalle St., Suite 900
Chicago IL 60601 U.S.A.

Kaleidoscope ISBNs
978-1-64519-033-2 (library bound)
978-1-64494-240-6 (paperback)
978-1-64519-133-9 (ebook)

World Book ISBN
978-0-7166-4334-0 (library bound)

Library of Congress Control Number
2019940250

Printed in the United States of America.

FIND ME IF YOU CAN!

Bigfoot lurks within one of the images in this book. It's up to you to find him!

TABLE OF
CONTENTS

CHAPTER 1

TAKING THE TESLA MODEL S FOR A RIDE

Eric was excited. His hands were sweaty. He was about to drive a Tesla Model S. He'd never done it before. This was an electric car. People said it was powerful. Now he would find out if that was true.

Another car was next to him. Eric looked at the driver. Who would be fastest? Eric tapped the screen on the **dashboard**. This let him change the car's controls. He tapped "Ludicrous" mode. The Model S was the quickest production car. No other car could **accelerate** faster. This was the fastest mode. He couldn't wait to try it.

Tesla made the first luxury electric car.

PARTS OF A
TESLA MODEL S

FUN FACT

The charging port door closes automatically when the car is unplugged.

Tesla logo

custom headlights

A man stood on the track. He held a green flag. Eric watched him. The man lowered the flag. Eric jammed his foot down. The motor had been **idling**. It had been quiet. Now it roared. It had a high-pitched whine. That was different. Other cars had a low growling sound.

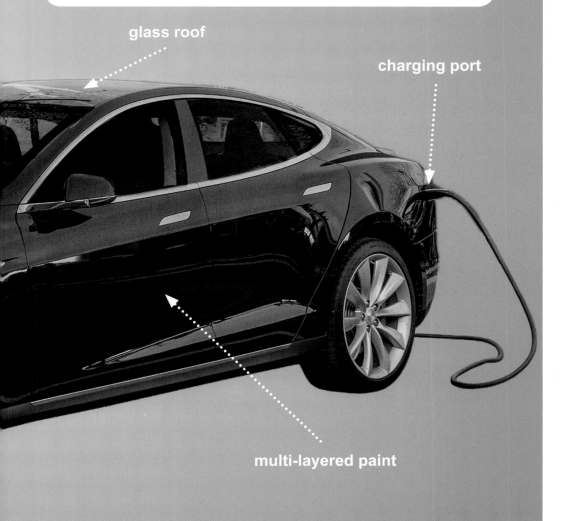

glass roof

charging port

multi-layered paint

Drivers choose Ludicrous mode on the display screen. After a warning, they click "Yes, bring it on!" to activate it.

The Model S leaped forward. It reached 60 miles per hour (97 km/h). This took just 2.4 seconds. And it kept speeding up. The Model S really was quick! Eric pulled ahead of the other car. It only took seconds. He was so excited. He shouted, "Woo-hoo!"

HOW TESLA GOT ITS NAME

Tesla is named after Nikola Tesla. He was an inventor. We still use many of his inventions today. His work involved electricity and motors. But he ran out of money. He couldn't finish all his plans. Martin Eberhard is one of Tesla's founders. He wanted to honor the inventor. Tesla invented a type of electric motor. The company uses this motor in its cars.

Tesla proved electric cars can be fast, powerful, and luxurious.

CHAPTER 2

HISTORY OF THE MODEL S

Elon Musk liked to create things. He started new companies. He created PayPal and SpaceX. He was also interested in electric cars.

One day, he got a phone call. It was from two engineers. One was named Martin Eberhard. The other was Marc Tarpenning. They had started a company. It was called Tesla. They told Musk about their work. They made electric cars. That was in 2004. Musk was excited. He wanted to be involved. Musk **invested** millions of dollars. He became one of Tesla's leaders. Musk wanted to build a great car. It had to be fun to drive.

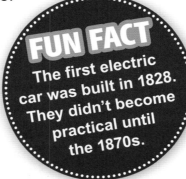

FUN FACT

The first electric car was built in 1828. They didn't become practical until the 1870s.

Elon Musk became the CEO of Tesla in 2008.

The Tesla factory is in Fremont, California.

Tesla revealed its first car in 2006. It shipped to customers in 2008. It became popular. Tesla started work on a new version. It would be the first electric luxury car. Luxury cars go fast. They are expensive. Other electric cars were being developed. But they were not stylish and fun. Tesla's would be. In 2012, Tesla released the Model S.

Electric cars run on batteries. They do not need gas. But they do need to recharge. People would need charging stations. Tesla began building them in 2012. They're called Superchargers. Superchargers charge a car's batteries. There are stations all over the world.

There are over 12,000 Superchargers around the world.

The Model S got an upgrade in 2014. It was a new feature. The feature was called Autopilot. This allowed the car to drive on its own. But there was a catch. It was not completely independent. Drivers had to keep their hands on the wheel. They had to take control if there was a problem.

Tesla keeps improving its cars. It wants them to be great. One problem was how far they could go. The early Model S could go around 208 miles (335 km). The range depended on how fast the car was traveling. Then it needed to recharge. Tesla worked on the batteries. Newer versions can go 335 miles (539 km).

Tesla also wants to find ways to lower costs. The cars are expensive. Tesla wants to make them cheaper. Then more people could drive one.

FUN FACT
Electric cars were more popular than gas cars until the 1920s.

Where the Tesla Model S Is Made

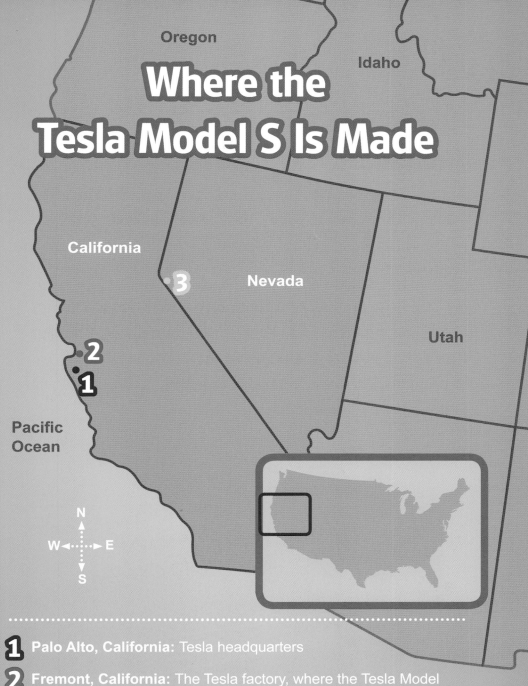

Oregon

Idaho

California

Nevada

3

Utah

2

1

Pacific
Ocean

N
W ◄┄┄► E
S

1 **Palo Alto, California:** Tesla headquarters

2 **Fremont, California:** The Tesla factory, where the Tesla Model S is assembled

3 **Sparks, Nevada:** The Tesla Gigafactory, where Tesla batteries are built

CHAPTER 3

WHAT MAKES THE MODEL S SPECIAL

Ashley loved her job. She worked at a Tesla **dealership**. Selling Tesla cars was fun. They were different. She enjoyed talking about the Model S. People came to see the cool car.

She showed the Model S to a couple. They wanted to know about its features. Ashley told them about Autopilot. She talked about the electric motor. The couple was impressed. They knew other companies made electric cars. But Ashley had something else to share.

There are Tesla showrooms all around the world.

THE TESLA MODEL S

IN DETAIL

Height: 4.7 feet (1.4 m)

Width: 7.2 feet (2.2 m)

COST: $79,000

Length: 16.3 feet (5 m)

Weight: 4,647 pounds (2,108 kg)

Top Speed: 155 miles per hour (249 km/h)

Time from 0–60 miles per hour (0–97 km/h): 2.4 seconds on Performance model

Each Tesla has software. The car's computer connects to the internet. Then the car can update its software. It's like a phone update. A screen in the car sends the owner a message. The owner can install the update when they're ready.

Ashley said this was unique. Other companies didn't make it so easy. The drivers had to bring their cars in for service. But Tesla drivers could update whenever they wanted. They could even do it at home.

FUN FACT
The Long Range model can go 335 miles (539 km) on a single charge!

The Model S has an extra trunk in the front of the car. Tesla calls it a "frunk."

Electric cars are an important step toward a future with cleaner energy.

The couple liked this. Ashley described the latest update. The Model S would have **obstacle**-aware acceleration. The car could detect something in front of it. Then it would slow down. It also had **blind spot** monitoring. This helped drivers change lanes. It would tell drivers when another car was in the way. These features made the car safer.

Ashley knew Tesla would continue **innovating**. Electric cars were the future. She couldn't wait to see what would come next.

FUN FACT

In Autopilot, the Model S changes lanes automatically when the turn signal is on.

CHAPTER 4

The Tesla Model S was the first electric car to go 300 miles (483 km) without recharging.

A CAR FROM THE FUTURE

Jason couldn't believe it. He was about to do something crazy. Jason stood in his driveway. A Model S was parked in his garage. It had Autopilot. Jason sent a message to the car. He used his phone. The message went to the car's computer. It started the Summon feature. The motor started. The car pulled out of the garage. Sensors noticed how close it was to the wall. The steering wheel moved on its own. The car stayed straight. It backed down the driveway. It stopped in front of him.

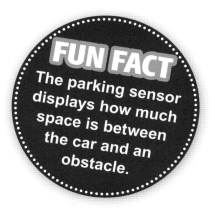

FUN FACT
The parking sensor displays how much space is between the car and an obstacle.

It was amazing. Jason had never seen anything like it. He got in. He buckled his seat belt. There was a large screen on the dashboard. He typed in his destination. He started driving. He had to drive on his own at first. Autopilot can't drive in cities. But then he reached the highway. He had to keep his hands on the wheel. But the car was driving itself. It knew where to go on its own. The car used computers and cameras. It followed a map. It could even change lanes. But then it left the highway. Jason had to take over.

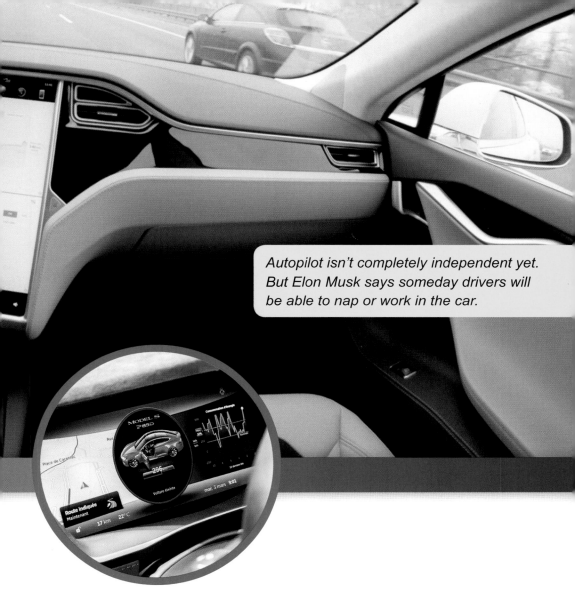

Autopilot isn't completely independent yet. But Elon Musk says someday drivers will be able to nap or work in the car.

In 2019, Elon Musk made a big announcement. He hoped Tesla would be fully self-driving soon. He said a driver could nap in the front seat! The car would do everything. Jason couldn't wait. He hoped Musk was right. He wanted to try it.

Jason kept driving. He thought about the car. He had learned many things about it. An electric motor powered it. Similar motors were being tested in race cars. These cars could go very fast. They had reached 300 miles per hour (483 km/h). That was a world record. Jason wished he could buy one. But they were not for sale yet.

Electric cars were efficient. They were also fast. Driving a Tesla was fun, too. It could even drive itself. Jason felt like he was driving in the future. It was an exciting place to be.

GAS VS. ELECTRIC MOTORS

An electric motor is more efficient than a gas engine. An engine needs a transmission. This moves the vehicle. It sends power to a car's wheels. As the car goes faster, the wheels need more power. An electric motor does not need a transmission. The electric car moves forward more quickly.

Tesla paved the way for electric cars to become popular for all kinds of people.

BEYOND
THE BOOK

After reading the book, it's time to think about what you learned. Try the following exercises to jumpstart your ideas.

THINK

DIFFERENT SOURCES. Think about what types of sources you could find on the Tesla Model S. What could you learn at a car dealership? What might you find in a magazine? How could each of the sources be useful in its own way?

CREATE

SHARPEN YOUR RESEARCH SKILLS. Tesla is the first company to develop an all-electric luxury car. Where could you go to find more information about that? Create a research plan. Then write a paragraph about your next steps.

SHARE

SUM IT UP. Write one paragraph summarizing the important points from this book. Make sure it's in your own words. Don't just copy what is in the text. Share the paragraph with a classmate. Does your classmate have any comments about your summary? Do they have additional questions about the Tesla Model S?

GROW

DRAWING CONNECTIONS. Create a drawing that shows the connections between the Tesla Model S and electricity. How has electricity shaped the history of electric cars? How does learning about electricity help you better understand the Tesla Model S?

RESEARCH NINJA

Visit *www.ninjaresearcher.com/0332* to learn how to take your research skills and book report writing to the next level!

RESEARCH

DIGITAL LITERACY TOOLS

SEARCH LIKE A PRO
Learn about how to use search engines to find useful websites.

FACT OR FAKE?
Discover how you can tell a trusted website from an untrustworthy resource.

TEXT DETECTIVE
Explore how to zero in on the information you need most.

SHOW YOUR WORK
Research responsibly— learn how to cite sources.

WRITE

GET TO THE POINT
Learn how to express your main ideas.

PLAN OF ATTACK
Learn prewriting exercises and create an outline.

DOWNLOADABLE REPORT FORMS

FURTHER RESOURCES

BOOKS

Eschbach, Christina. *Inside Electric Cars*. Abdo Publishing, 2019.

Murray, Julie. *Tesla Model S*. Abdo Publishing, 2018.

Oachs, Emily Rose. *Tesla Model S*. Bellwether Media, 2018.

WEBSITES

FACTSURFER

Factsurfer.com gives you a safe, fun way to find more information.

1. Go to www.factsurfer.com.

2. Enter "Tesla Model S" into the search box and click 🔍.

3. Select your book cover to see a list of related websites.

GLOSSARY

accelerate: To accelerate means to go faster. The Tesla Model S can accelerate very quickly.

blind spot: A blind spot is an area around a vehicle that the driver cannot see while driving. The Tesla Model S has many cameras that monitor the car's blind spots.

dashboard: The dashboard is the front part of a car that has the controls and displays on it. The dashboard has the speedometer and GPS screen.

dealership: A car dealership sells a specific brand of cars. The Tesla Model S can be found at a Tesla dealership.

idling: Something that is idling is not moving or being used. The Tesla Model S motor is quiet while it is idling.

innovating: Innovating means finding new ways to do or make things. Tesla worked at innovating a self-driving feature for the Model S.

invested: When people have invested, they have put money into something with plans to earn more money. Elon Musk invested several million dollars in Tesla.

obstacle: An obstacle blocks a path. The Tesla Model S has cameras that can see an obstacle in the road.

transmission: The transmission is the part of a vehicle that uses power from gasoline to turn the wheels. The Tesla Model S does not use gasoline and does not have a transmission.

INDEX

PHOTO CREDITS

ABOUT THE AUTHOR

Amy C. Rea grew up in northern Minnesota and now lives in a Minneapolis suburb with her husband, two sons, and dog. She writes frequently about traveling around Minnesota.